TEENS IN INDIA

Global
connections

Teens in India

by Lori Shores

Content Adviser: Anu Taranath, Ph.D.,
Department of English,
University of Washington, Seattle

Reading Adviser: Katie Van Sluys, Ph.D.,
Department of Teacher Education,
DePaul University

Compass Point Books Minneapolis, Minnesota

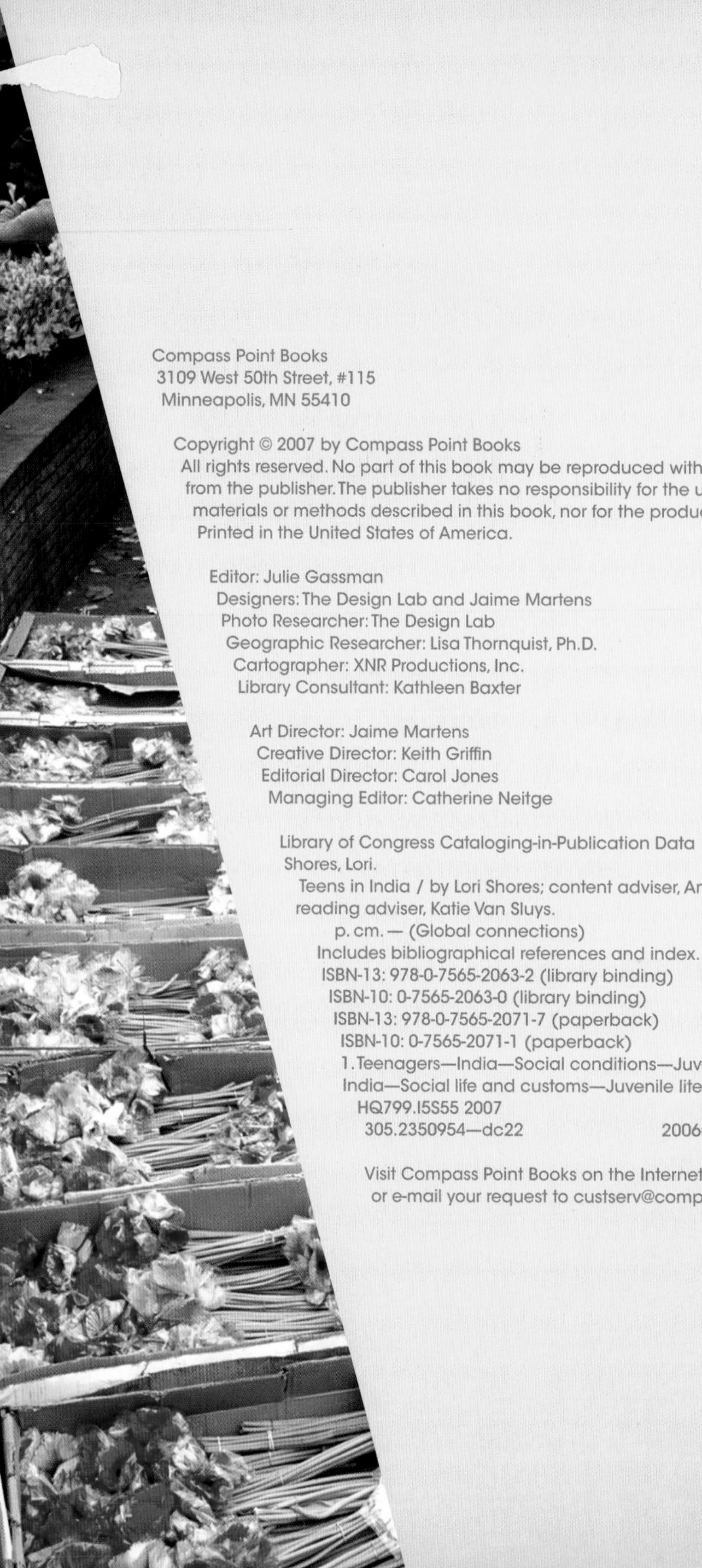

Compass Point Books
3109 West 50th Street, #115
Minneapolis, MN 55410

Printed in the United States of America.

Editor: Julie Gassman
Designers: The Design Lab and Jaime Martens
Photo Researcher: The Design Lab
Geographic Researcher: Lisa Thornquist, Ph.D.
Cartographer: XNR Productions, Inc.
Library Consultant: Kathleen Baxter

Art Director: Jaime Martens
Creative Director: Keith Griffin
Editorial Director: Carol Jones
Managing Editor: Catherine Neitge

Library of Congress Cataloging-in-Publication Data
Shores, Lori.
Teens in India / by Lori Shores; content adviser, Anu Taranath; reading adviser, Katie Van Sluys.
p. cm. — (Global connections)
Includes bibliographical references and index.
ISBN-13: 978-0-7565-2063-2 (library binding)
ISBN-10: 0-7565-2063-0 (library binding)
ISBN-13: 978-0-7565-2071-7 (paperback)
ISBN-10: 0-7565-2071-1 (paperback)
1. Teenagers—India—Social conditions—Juvenile literature. 2. Teenagers—India—Social life and customs—Juvenile literature. I. Title. II. Series.
HQ799.I5S55 2007
305.2350954—dc22 2006005299

Visit Compass Point Books on the Internet at www.compasspointbooks.com
or e-mail your request to custserv@compasspointbooks.com.

Table of Contents

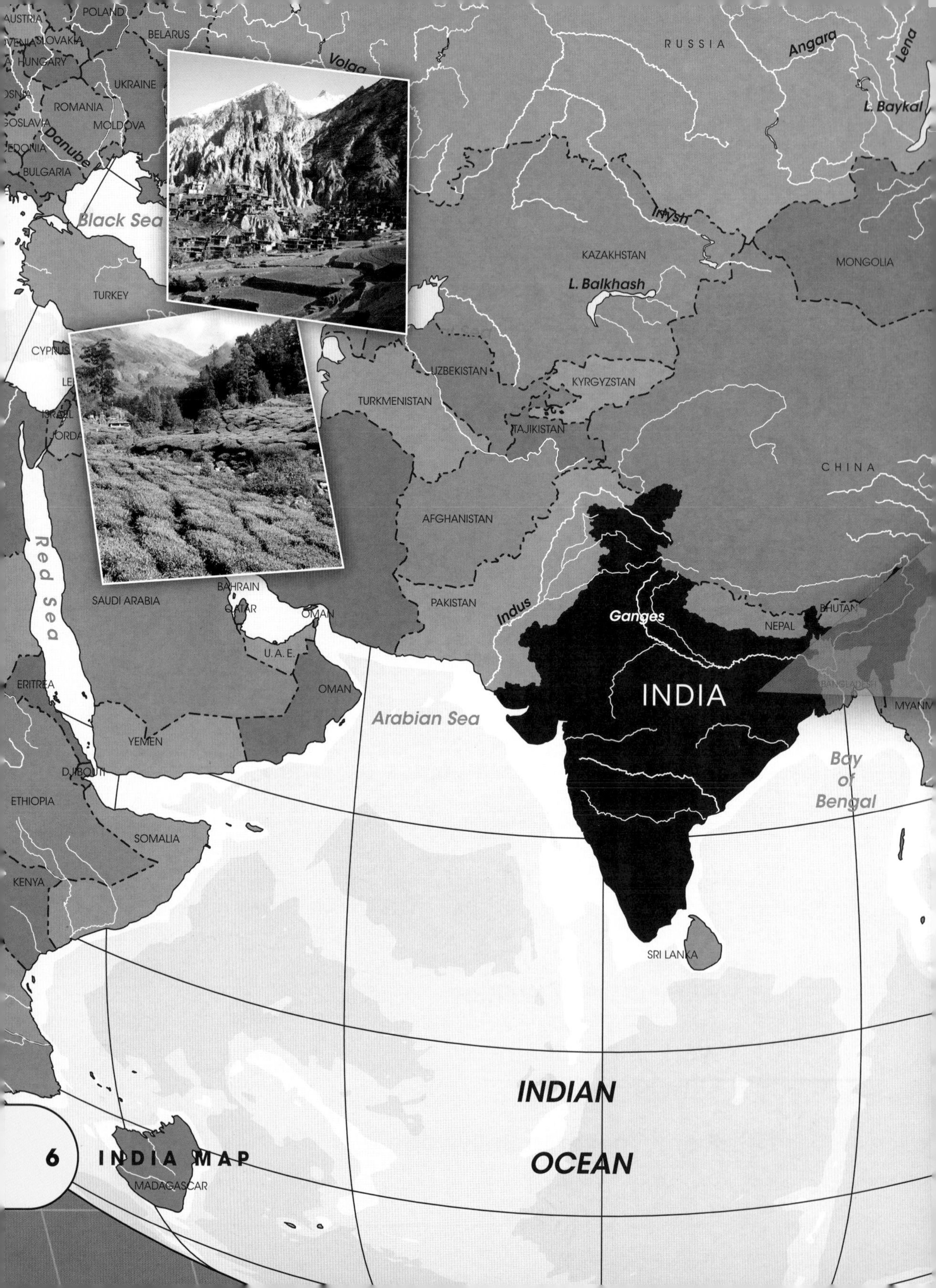
POLAND
AUSTRIA
SLOVAKIA
HUNGARY
BELARUS
UKRAINE
ROMANIA
MOLDOVA
Danube
BULGARIA
Black Sea
TURKEY
CYPRUS
ISRAEL
Volga
RUSSIA
Angara
Lena
L. Baykal
Irtysh
KAZAKHSTAN
L. Balkhash
MONGOLIA
UZBEKISTAN
KYRGYZSTAN
TURKMENISTAN
TAJIKISTAN
CHINA
AFGHANISTAN
Red Sea
SAUDI ARABIA
BAHRAIN
QATAR
OMAN
U.A.E.
PAKISTAN
Indus
Ganges
NEPAL
BHUTAN
BANGLADESH
INDIA
ERITREA
YEMEN
Arabian Sea
Bay of Bengal
DJIBOUTI
ETHIOPIA
SOMALIA
KENYA
SRI LANKA
INDIAN OCEAN
MADAGASCAR

Sea
of Japan
JAPAN
NORTH KOREA
SOUTH KOREA
Huang
Yellow
Sea
New Delhi
Yangtze
PHILIPPINES
VIETNAM
LAOS
South
China
Sea
THAILAND
Mekong
KAMPUCHEA
INDONESIA
BRUNEI
MALAYSIA
MALAYSIA
SINGAPORE
INDONESIA

THE REPUBLIC OF INDIA IS HOME TO MORE THAN 411 MILLION YOUNG PEOPLE, AGES 6 TO 24. It is also home to some of the most ancient civilizations, including four major world religions. The country's diversity can be seen in the experience of Indian teens, which is anything but dull. For many teens, attending school and earning good grades is the most important activity, since education is highly valued. Other teens work hard on the family farm or in homes of the upper class to help support their families.

But there's more to teen life in India than good grades and hard work. Teens enjoy a wide variety of activities, from singing and dancing in after-school clubs to playing cricket. On any given day, teens can be found chatting in cafes, riding bikes, or simply lounging in the late afternoon sun. While Indian teens may be among the busiest teens in the world, they still find time to have fun and relax with their friends and family.

Students at a secondary school in Port Blair were happy to be in class after schools were closed for 10 days following a devastating tsunami in December 2004.

1

CHAPTER ONE

School Days & Ways

WITH NEARLY 31 PERCENT OF THE POPULATION UNDER AGE 15, THE INDIAN GOVERNMENT views its youth as a valuable resource. This makes the education of youth of utmost importance. Indian students attend classes nearly year-round, from April until the beginning of March. Their monthlong vacation falls at the end of the Indian winter.

This full schedule is due in part to the many days schools are closed for national and religious holidays each year. More important, however, it is a reflection of the government's dedication to the education of its young people.

There are more than 1 million schools in India, not counting colleges and universities. More than

Indian School Structure

Primary

Grades	Ages
1-5	6-11

Upper Primary

Grades	Ages
6-9	11-14

Secondary

Grades	Ages
10-12	14-18

90 percent of primary schools and 72 percent of upper primary schools are publicly funded, while an estimated 61 percent of secondary schools are privately funded.

These secondary schools are often run by religious organizations, such as churches and missionary institutions. Others are privately operated with grant money from the government. Even with funding from the government or private institutions, private education is an expense afforded only by the upper and upper-middle economic classes.

Who's Going to School?

Though schooling is mandatory and public schools are free, there is a high dropout rate among teens in India. In the 1990s, it was estimated that only about 50 percent of children were enrolled in school, and a later estimate by India's Ministry of Human Resource Development showed a dropout rate of more than 62 percent in secondary schools. These figures reflect the fact that many children and teens who should be in school are working instead.

According to a column in *Business Standard*, an Indian magazine, these figures also reflect other problems of the culture. Columnist Sumita Kale writes:

Students at a Catholic school in the state of Meghalaya begin each day with a morning meeting. Many people in the northeast states are Christian.

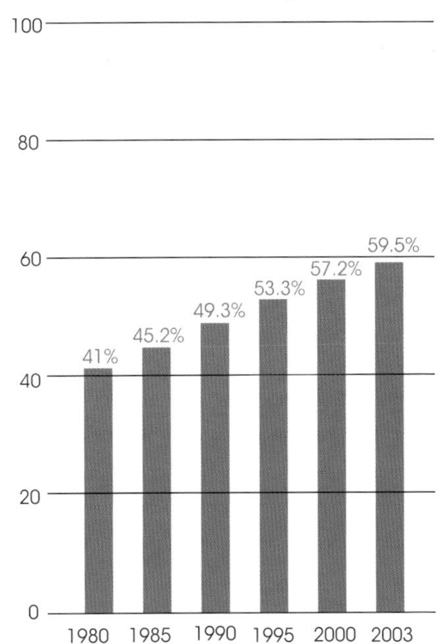

Source: U.N. Common Database.

Who's Reading

In order to help people learn to read, the Indian government began a literacy campaign in 1993. The program makes use of nearly 10 million volunteer teachers. This effort places a special focus on improving literacy among the female population.

A 2003 study found the adult literacy rate in India to be 59.5 percent, with a large gap between the males (70.2 percent) and females (48.3 percent) because of gender discrimination. Still, these figures reflect improvement since 1995, when the literacy rates were 63.9 percent for males and 39.4 percent for females.

Some child workers sell items or provide services like shoe shining on the city streets.

"High drop-out and low attendance rates are all complex problems connected to deeper concerns of gender, class, caste structure and poverty."

In rural areas, children may be enrolled in school, since it is mandatory, but never actually attend. Indian law prohibits children, including teens, from working in factories. It does, however, allow for the employment of children in family households, restaurants, or agriculture. Because 25 percent of the population lives in poverty, young children and teens often must work instead of attending school. They need to help provide for the family.

Boys and girls attend separate classes and sometimes separate schools. On average, each class consists of around 50 students. Since classes are so large, students do not leave the classroom at the end of a period to go to their next subject.

Teen Scenes

A group of teens sits outside a favorite café in the city, enjoying the cool breeze of the evening. Their week has been jampacked with studies and exam preparation, but now the friends can relax, share tea, and gossip. As a red double-decker bus roars by, the teens can smell the hot dust stirred up in its wake, and for a moment their conversation is interrupted. Soon they are back to giggling and storytelling. They ignore the noise and commotion on the busy city street as they enjoy their valued free time before heading home to dinner with their families ... and maybe a little more studying.

In another corner of the city, a group of teens is busy at work, sewing small crystals onto luxurious fabric. Though it is illegal to employ children under 14, some of the factory workers haven't reached their teen years. Their families depend on them to earn what they can to help the household. And school has to be forgotten to allow time for work. When their days are over, they can escape to their family homes for rest and maybe a game of cricket.

Far away from the city, a village teen awakes from a short nap in the afternoon sun. His day, too, has been filled with labor, but his work differs greatly from city work. He has worked alongside his family members, tending their field. Rushing home along a path, he imagines the sounds awaiting him at home—the butter spattering as his mother fries small packets of meat and vegetables, his father's deep voice singing a traditional song, and his young siblings playing in the yard.

While some teens spend their days studying and preparing for exams, others labor, perhaps in city factories or on country farms. When the work is done in the evening, teens all across the country can look back on a productive day and enjoy some time of rest. From the city to the village, teens find their own ways of winding down before another busy day.

Who's in Charge?

During the 18th and 19th centuries, traders from several European countries arrived in India and later established colonies in the country. By 1856, most of India was under the control of the British East India Company. A year later, the Indian Rebellion broke out, but the effort for independence failed, and India became a colony of the British Empire. As is common during colonization, the British exploited the Indian people and the country's resources.

In the early 20th century, a nationwide struggle for independence was launched by the Indian National Congress, led by Mohandas Gandhi. Millions of people engaged in protests with a commitment to ahimsa, or nonviolence. On August 15, 1947, India finally gained independence from British rule. Three years later, on January 26, 1950, India chose to be a republic, and a new constitution was written.

In Devannapet, Andhra Pradesh, students are taught the regional Telegu language in addition to Hindi and English.

Instead, they stay in the same classroom all day with various teachers coming and going each hour. The exception to this is for physical education, a requirement for all students in India. Once a week, students learn exercises and play games as part of their physical education. It is a welcome change in the routine of their school week.

Classes & Coursework

Here's a look at some of the topics covered in the math, science, and social science courses.

MATH	SCIENCE	SOCIAL SCIENCE
Commercial mathematics—problems on percentages, profit and loss, discount, and compound interest	**Nature and behavior of matter**—structure of atoms, periodic classification of elements, and chemical bonding and reactions	**Contemporary world**—rise of colonialism, the Russian Revolution, the rise of fascism and Nazism, and World Wars I and II
Geometry—problems using lines and angles, parallelograms, area, and construction of triangles	**Motion, force, and work**—gravitation, energy, and wave motion	**Making of a modern world**—constitution of India and Indian democracy
Statistics—frequency tables, graphical representation of data, and averages	**Living world**—cell structure; tissues; food, nutrition, and health; and human diseases	**Land and people**—climate, drainage, natural vegetation and wildlife, population, and disaster management in India
	Natural resources—coal, petroleum, and sustainable agriculture	
	Environment—habitat, adaptation in plants and animals, ecological system, and causes and effects of changes in habitats	

Source: Central Board of Education, New Delhi, India.

So Much to Learn!

There are 18 official languages in India, and they are spoken in more than 1,600 distinct dialects. The official modern language of India is Hindi. English is also widely spoken as a result of the long period of British rule. Because of the number of languages spoken in the country, teens normally take at least three language courses: English,

A Typical School Day

Schools in India usually start around 8 A.M., sometimes with a short assembly period during which students are given moral instruction and information about current events. Regular classes are generally 40 minutes long, and a typical school day consists of eight classes.

Some schools offer a break for lunch, while others offer only occasional, short breaks for students to get out of their chairs and stretch a bit.

modern Indian language (Hindi), and a regional language, such as Bengali or Urdu. Language courses vary widely, depending on where they are taken.

Other courses for Indian teens include mathematics, technology and science, social sciences, health, and art. As they get older and progress through their education, teens have more choices for elective courses. This allows them more freedom to choose courses that they will enjoy and that will prepare them for their careers. In grades 11 and 12, there are three main areas of study from which to choose electives: science, commerce, and humanities.

Courses in science may include information technology, computer programming, or electronics. Computer use in primary and secondary schools is growing in India as the information technology field broadens. Though many schools are in need of simple things like blackboards, according to an article in an Indian daily newspaper, "more than 93,000 schools imparting elementary education had computers in place." Students who choose science courses are likely preparing for further study in these areas in college.

In commerce, students may learn bookkeeping and accounting, or other financial education. These courses help them prepare for college coursework toward a degree in business. In the area of humanities, students may

Students often contribute to public holiday celebrations and spend time at school preparing for them.

study literature, art, music, or dance. Because these studies are not viewed as advantageous in the job market, they may be frowned upon by parents who want their children to enter more profitable careers.

Extracurricular Activities

Teenagers are encouraged to participate in school clubs and organizations, and in some schools these activities are mandatory. Even if participation is required, there is little pressure to perform well. School coursework and grades are the most important aspects of their education.

There are many options for teens choosing extracurricular activities, ranging from sports like cricket and soccer to singing and dancing clubs. Some of the most popular activities are drama club, music club, and student government. Students are also encouraged to take part in other school activities, such as plays and performances.

Some schools participate in large contests, which are called fests. The fests often include many types of competitions, ranging from academic activities like debate and oration to outdoor athletic events. These contests are very popular with teens who look forward to meeting and socializing with students from other

Traditional dance contests are part of the high school competitions.

Students often squeeze in some last-minute studying before exams.

schools—especially those attending all-boys and all-girls schools. The students often spend the hours after school preparing for these events, practicing more and more until the day the performance or competition finally arrives.

On the day of a fest, there is much commotion and excitement as students rush from one activity to another. Students who are not participating in contests still attend to support and cheer on their friends. While a cricket match takes place outside in the hot sun, performances are held inside the auditorium. Both activities get equal attention and support.

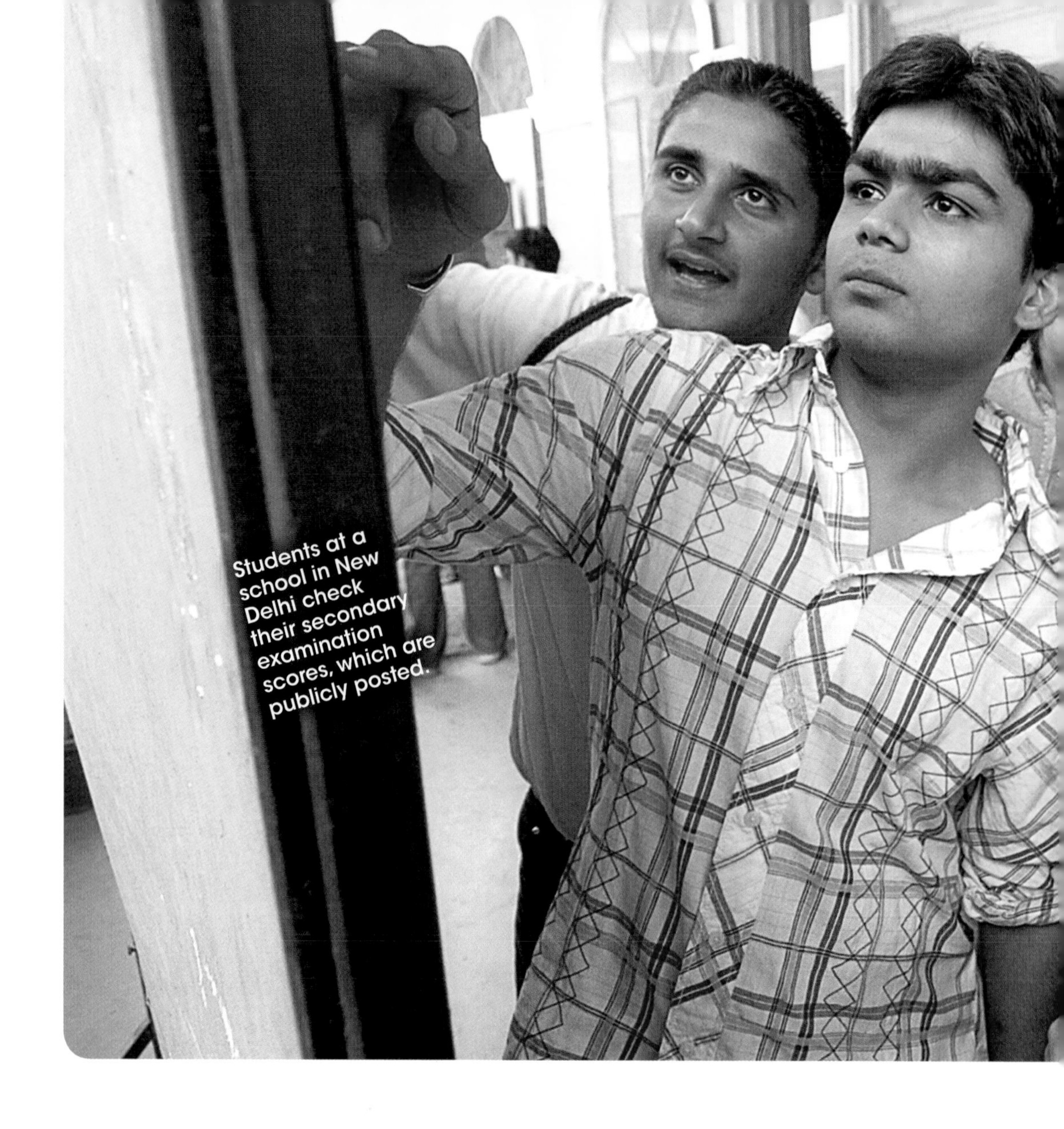
Students at a school in New Delhi check their secondary examination scores, which are publicly posted.

At the end of the 12th grade, students enjoy a special end-of-school celebration. On prize distribution day, as it is called, awards are given to students who have done especially well on exams and in other school activities.

Students also pass around their school magazines for friends to sign at the end of the year. These magazines are produced by the students, with help from teachers who review and edit material. In addition to photographs,

school magazines contain student-submitted writing and artwork. In the end, each student has a magazine filled with memories of the current school year to treasure.

Good Grades & School Success

Teens feel significant pressure to do well in school. Both teachers and parents who want their children to be prepared for technical and professional careers stress the importance of education. Because most students who stay in school plan to attend college, they take their studies seriously and spend a great deal of their time preparing for their exams. Most often, the measure of success in school is exam grades. Students need to study for weekly, midterm, and end-of-semester exams. In addition, teachers assign a large amount of daily homework.

As if the daily homework and frequent tests weren't stressful enough, there are two major tests all students must take to gain entrance to a college or university. Competition to get into even an average college can be high, so teens study hard to get high marks on these exams.

Many students take extra courses for a fee after school in preparation for exams. Sometimes these tuition classes, as they are called, begin right after school is dismissed. Students have no time to return home for lunch or an after-school snack. Tuition courses are not only for exam preparation. Some teens study subjects like music or athletics, reflecting their parents' desire for them to do well not only in academics but also in other areas.

It is not uncommon to see elephants roaming throughout the country.

CHAPTER TWO

2 Day In & Day Out

A TYPICAL DAY FOR INDIAN TEENS starts as early as 6 A.M., when they get up and get ready for school. Styling hair doesn't take long for either the boys, who generally wear their hair short, or the girls, who usually pull their long hair back in a braid or casual ponytail. As for makeup, most Indian girls don't worry about it. Makeup is seen as something women, not girls, use.

Teens of the middle and upper classes who attend private schools may dress in plaid school uniforms for their busy day. Those who attend schools without uniforms will usually dress in Indian clothing. Girls often wear a sari, a long piece of fabric that is draped around the body in various ways. One common way to wear a sari is to wrap it around the waist and up over a shoulder. Despite the rise in popularity of Western fashions, the sari—called by some "the world's most graceful attire"—is a favorite choice for many young women. There are numerous styles of sari fabric, ranging from cotton in a solid color to ornate and intricately decorated silk.

The cloth of a sari drapes down the back.

Fashion Corner

Many young women like to wear imported Western fashions such as jeans and T-shirts. The foreign brands Reebok and Nike are especially popular among teens. Several Indian companies make and sell Westernized fashions as well.

While they may enjoy Western fashions, teens wear Indian clothing for important festivals, holidays, and other family events.

Another popular choice for girls is the *salwar kameez*, a long tunic worn over drawstring pants. An important piece of the kameez is the *dupatta*, a long scarf usually worn around the neck and draped down the back. This scarf, like the excess material of the sari, can be used to cover the head in temples or in front of elders as a way to show respect. Muslim women and girls often wear a burkha, a loose garment that is long enough to cover them from head to foot, and is usually black.

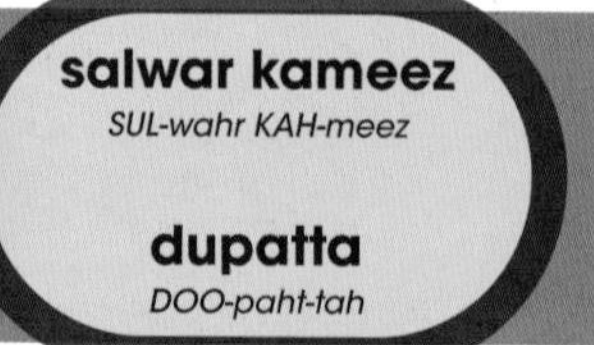

salwar kameez
SUL-wahr KAH-meez

dupatta
DOO-paht-tah

Boys in India wear pants and shirts similar to Western styles. Or boys wear a kurta, a long shirt that hangs below the beltline, with loose pants. There are many styles of kurta, some made with fine linen and silk and others made of simple cotton. Most kurta have three or four buttons at the neck and are decorated around the buttons and cuffs with embroidery or painted designs. Some boys wear a dhoti, which is a loose white garment worn pulled up between the legs like a long loincloth.

Male followers of the Sikh religion, which was founded in northern India during the 16th century, wear turbans. The turbans show their love and devotion to their faith and its founders.

A typical agricultural duty is picking cotton. India produces more cotton than any other country.

The Day Ahead

By 7 A.M., when they are dressed and groomed, teens eat a breakfast of rice left over from the previous evening's meal. Another option is a pancake made of rice and lentils—staples in the Indian diet. Next it is off to school on either a school bus or a public bus.

After their seven- or eight-hour school day, teens head home to have a late lunch, typically rice and lentils, if they did not eat at school. After lunch, most teens study and complete their homework. While some teens manage to find time to play games with their friends in the neighborhood, they are normally too busy with their studies and extracurricular activities to have much time to socialize after school.

Children and teens also have household chores and responsibilities. Around the age of 5 or 6, children in rural areas learn to help with the agricultural duties of the family. In cities, too, children and teens learn household duties, recognizing their importance in the structure and success of the family. Most girls are taught domestic chores. Boys, meanwhile, help with the physical labor of the family agricultural work, even if only in backyard gardens. It is normal for teens to help the family in both domestic and agricultural work. They do not expect an allowance for helping their family.

In villages around the country, both boys and girls are expected to help with daily agricultural tasks such as weeding. During harvest time, teens work alongside their elders to help with the difficult work of harvesting and threshing. Indian teens are expected to contribute to household and family duties.

Another important responsibility for many teenagers in India is caring for younger siblings. In extended families, which usually consist of many generations living together, relatives take turns playing with and caring for the young ones.

Many teens spend time with their younger siblings and cousins. They play a large role in their care, including feeding and bathing them. Even in nuclear families with just two or three children, teens often help care for younger siblings. It is common to see young people carrying little siblings with them as they go about their business in the home or on errands.

By helping care for younger siblings, teens build close relationships with their brothers and sisters.

A Look at Hinduism

Though more than 80 percent of its population is Hindu, India is a secular state, meaning there is no official national religion. Hinduism embodies a wide range of beliefs and practices and is said to be "the only major religion in the world that does not claim to be the only true religion." Hinduism dominates India's culture and forms the basis of many social and personal responsibilities and expectations. No discussion of the life of an Indian would be complete without a basic understanding of the principles of Hinduism.

Karma, Dharma, & Reincarnation

Central to Hindu faith is a belief in reincarnation. Hindus believe that the atman, or soul, lives many lives in various bodies, times, and places. In this regard, Hinduism can be seen as a religion that believes in second—or third, fourth, fifth, and even more—chances. The number of incarnations a soul may have is unlimited.

A Hindu priest lights a lantern by the Ganges River as part of a morning prayer offering.

Reincarnation is also a complex system of reward and punishment. Karma is the name given to conduct or actions in a previous life. For example, if in one life, a person does not live in a righteous manner, he or she may be born into a lower caste, or class, in the next life. Intentionally harming another person may come back to haunt the one who did it. The force of karma seeks to correct wrongs and balance the positive and negative energies of humanity.

In order to escape these unfavorable possibilities, Hindus try to live according to the laws of dharma, or appropriate behavior for one's station in life. Performing one's dharma increases the chances of being born again into a higher station in life. It is also a means of gaining self-knowledge that will help people eventually escape the cycle of birth and rebirth. Those who escape the cycle attain *moksha*, or liberation from the physical and material world.

The Hindu Trinity

Hindus worship thousands of gods, great and small, male and female. Don't worry for your Hindu friends, though—memorizing the names and attributes of every one of these gods and goddesses is unnecessary. Above all others, the three gods that make up the Hindu trinity are the most important to focus on in understanding the basics of Hinduism. The three gods of the trinity, known as the Trimurti, are Brahma, the Creator; Shiva, the Destroyer; and Vishnu, the Preserver. Each of these gods plays a distinct role and has its own personality and attributes. Together they make up Brahman, or The One, the ultimate reality that is God. Brahman is the source of all creation and is formless, without attributes, and eternal.

moksha
MOHK-shah

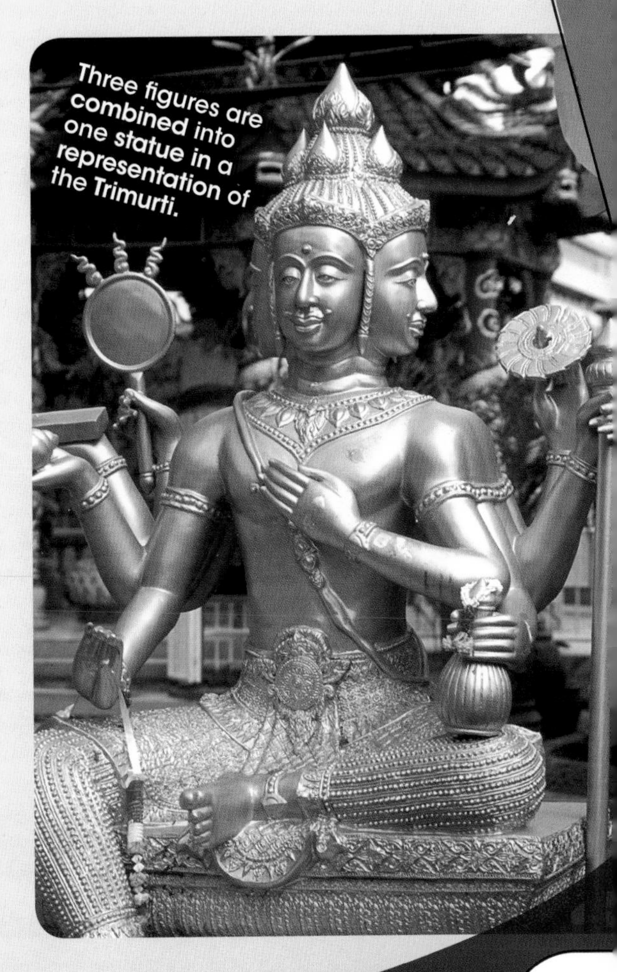
Three figures are combined into one statue in a representation of the Trimurti.

What's for Dinner?

Typically, an Indian family eats its evening meal between 7:30 and 9 P.M. Dinner usually includes rice, lentils, and possibly some sort of fried food, such as samosa, which are packets of a meat and/or vegetables, lentils, and spices. Few teens help with meal preparation, since Indian cuisine is quite complicated.

Vegetarianism is common throughout India, especially among Hindus. However, it is not the only diet followed. Among the Muslim population (about 14 percent of India), kebab (meat on a stick) and pilaf (mixtures of rice, meat, and vegetables) are standard fare, along with rich meat gravies served over rice or flat bread.

Teens usually eat their evening

Indian specialties include samosa (left) and curries (right). Flatbread often accompanies a meal.

Because the cow is sacred in Hindu culture, Indian McDonald's do not serve beef.

meal with their parents, and both parents and teens enjoy the same foods. Indian cuisine is by far the most popular choice for teens, even with McDonald's and Taco Bell restaurants popping up in large cities such as Bangalore and New Delhi. Among the middle and upper classes, teenagers have more food choices, and many enjoy Western cuisine such as hot dogs, pizza, and carbonated soft drinks. These foods are generally more expensive and seen as a luxury, so they are not available to teens in the lower economic classes.

Especially popular among Indian families is the Islam tradition of ending the evening meal with a sweet dessert, often made of almonds, rice, or coconut, and sweetened with sugar. With or without a formal dessert, though, many Indian meals are finished off with an after-dinner treat called *paan*. Paan is a heart-shaped leaf of the betel

Kulfi is ice cream that is flavored with the spices cardamom and saffron and has pistachio nuts. *Rasgulla* are balls made of cream cheese served in sweet syrup. *Gulab jamun* is another type of dessert ball. They are made of ground almonds and honey. *Firnee* is a very rich rice pudding.

kulfi
KOOL-fhee

rasgulla
RUS-goo-lah

gulab jamun
GOO-lahb JAH-moon

firnee
FEIR-nee

Paan is prepared and sold by vendors on the street.

creeper plant that is folded into a triangle with sweet ingredients and spices inside. The most common spices used in paan preparation are aniseed, cardamom, cloves, and areca nut—spices that aid in digestion. Other ingredients for an after-dinner paan can be betel nut, grated coconut, lime paste, or even a sweet jam. The after-dinner paan not only serves as a tasty treat and a digestion aid, but it also freshens breath.

Home Time

The family home, and especially the yard, is an important place for the family to gather for relaxation or for outdoor parties, such as weddings or holiday celebrations. In cities such as New Delhi, most families live in duplexes or houses with flat roofs and

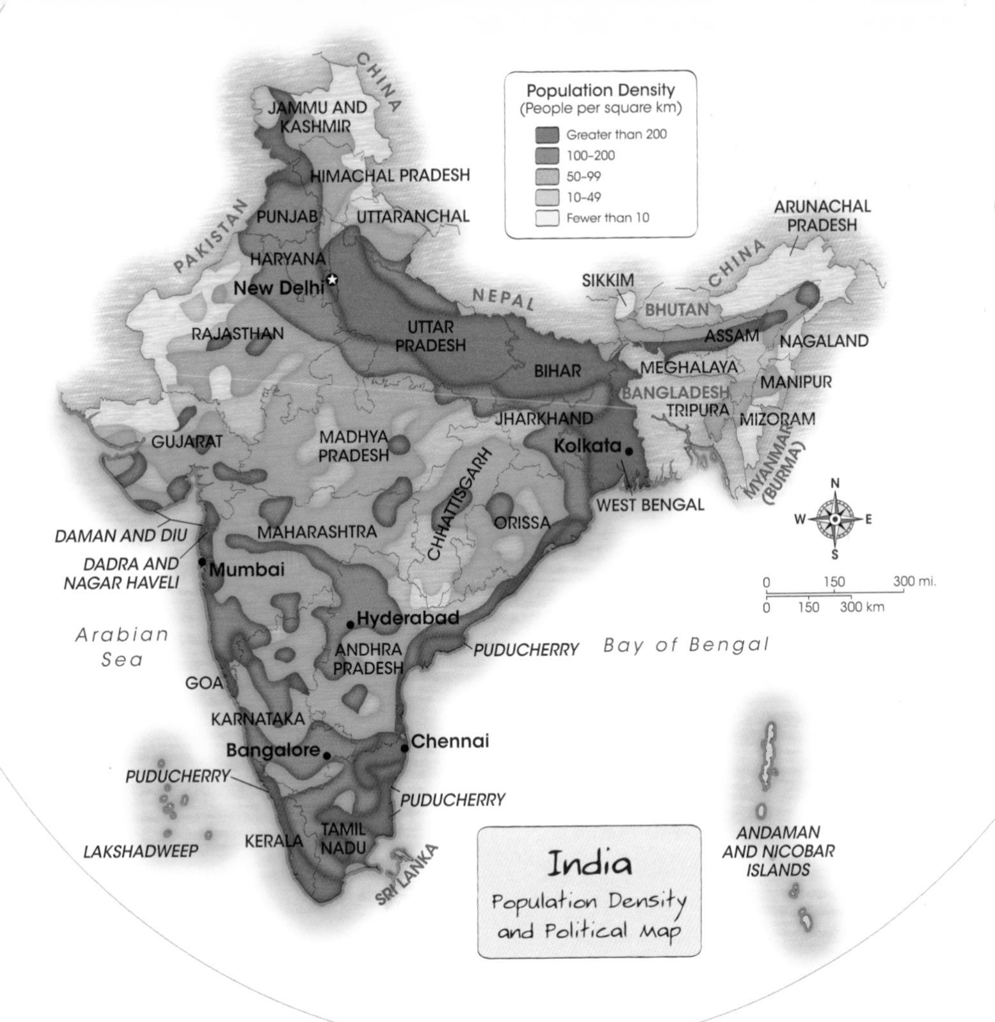

large yards where members can gather. Some cities, such as Mumbai, have very few houses. Instead there are many apartment complexes and duplexes that people rent.

In rural areas, where 72 percent of India's population lives, mud-plastered houses are common. These homes have dirt floors and walls made of packed mud, and they are often decorated with traditional designs. Rural landowners may live in concrete houses, while the people they employ to tend the land live in simple dwellings.

The number of rooms in a typical Indian home varies according to family structure. Many teens live with their parents, grandparents, aunts, uncles, and cousins in extended-family homes with as many as eight rooms. In contrast, homes for smaller nuclear families have only two or three rooms.

Teens usually share their bedrooms with siblings and possibly other family

Mud homes with thatched roofs need continual maintenance.

members. The main family phone is usually kept in the living room or in the parents' bedroom. The same is true for the family computer, for the small percentage of families who own one.

Poverty is common in Indian cities. The streets are packed with people of all classes, and it is common to see upper-class women dressed in lavish clothing and gold jewelry shopping alongside barefoot children who are waiting outside restaurants for scraps of food and donations of money. Grand homes of the wealthy are sometimes within walking distance of shabby huts of the poor that are covered with burlap to protect against wind and rain. Poor people often have nowhere else to live than on the paved city sidewalks and landings of apartment buildings.

In less prominent parts of the city, many homeless people find shelter together in open areas, where they can construct crude structures made of mud and tin sheeting. There streets and ditches are filled with raw sewage because the people and animals have no sanitary facilities available to them.

In Mumbai, a luxury high-rise towers above deteriorating housing for people with lower incomes.

Doorway Designs

Often the front entrances of Hindu homes are decorated daily with intricate designs drawn with rice-flour paste. Called *kolam* or *rangoli*, these designs are signs of welcome. The most common colors used are white and red, although any color other than black may be used. Some kolam are drawn with geometric shapes, and others have animals or flowers. Usually females create these designs. Teen girls can often be found decorating the threshold of their home with their beautiful creations.

kolam
KOH-lum

rangoli
RAHNG-oh-lee

These designs also convey messages from and about the family that dwells in the home. Some symbols may inform passing holy men that they are welcome to stop for food and drink. Other designs symbolize the wealth and success of the family. An added benefit of these designs, it is said, is that gods and goddesses are attracted by beautiful rangoli. They will cross the threshold to bestow good fortune and happiness on the family.

The average family has three children, though the number varies from state to state.

CHAPTER THREE

3 Family Ties

IN INDIA, FAMILY LIFE IS THE GUIDING FORCE OF A TEEN'S LIFE, FOR IT IS in the home that he or she learns the expectations of society. Family values—which are greatly respected and even considered sacred—are passed down through generations.

The family home provides a refuge at the end of the day. After dinner is eaten and dishes cleaned up, it is common for family members, and sometimes friends, to gather in front yards or on rooftops to relax, discuss their day, and enjoy one another's company.

Teens have close relationships with their parents and value their roles in their lives. Grandparents and other relatives are held in esteem as well.

Family Structure

In India, the extended family unit is common in both rural and urban areas. Often, two or more married couples from the same family will share a home and financial responsibilities.

In certain villages and city neighborhoods, when a couple marries they are expected to take up permanent residence with the family of either the bride or the groom. Usually the groom's family is the welcoming party, but this often depends on the religion of the family. Because each married couple then increases the family with an average of two to four children, the Indian home is a place of constant activity.

While it is by far the most common family structure, the intergenerational extended family is not the only type of family in India. In some areas, especially around the base of the Himalaya mountains, polygyny is common. In such families, a man may live with two wives and have children with each. In the mountain areas of Jammu and Kashmir, Buddhist families may consist of a set of brothers who share one or more wives. In this type of family, the brothers and sons will also share land and finances. The children of these families will then leave home to create their own families when they marry.

Families split by divorce and blended families—those consisting of two previously married or widowed parents and

What's In a Name

Common Names in India

Boys	Girls
Anand	Lakshmi
Anil	Aparna
Ajay	Parvati
Pramod	Sindhu
Abhishek	Lata
Halim	Ayesha

In the Himalaya region, women and children work together to earn money for the family.

their respective children—are uncommon in India. Divorce is rare in rural areas of India, though in urban areas it is increasing. Still, the divorce rate in India is among the lowest worldwide. A 2003 study showed only a 1.1 percent divorce rate, meaning 11 marriages in 1,000 end in divorce. In both Hindu and Islam, marriage is a sacred institution. Divorce is socially unacceptable, if permitted at all.

Sometimes young couples move out of the extended family home in order to find work in a city. Even in these situations, they normally still live near family. Groups of relatives usually live quite close to one another, even if

Global connections

Living the Holy Life

Not everyone in India remains close to family throughout life. A sadhu is a person, usually a man, who has given his entire life to spirituality. A sadhu cuts ties to his family and all social and material connections. He then spends his life in search of higher levels of spirituality through meditation, devotion, pilgrimages, and the study of sacred books. Rather than living in a house or an apartment, a sadhu wanders from town to town, accepting gifts of food and shelter from families he meets along the way.

A sadhu bathes in a river during a pilgrimage to a shrine.

Unlike most of India, the state of Meghalay is matriarchal, and women lead the family.

not in the same house. Strong bonds are formed by siblings and cousins in a family, and bickering among them is not common. It is hard to imagine a teen getting bored when there are so many people around to talk to and cousins to hang out with.

The Family Hierarchy

Within the family, there is an unmistakable order of importance and influence based on gender. The distinctions between men and women, and boys and girls, are very pronounced. Indian family life is predominantly patriarchal, as is common in 90 percent of the world's cultures.

The patriarch of the family, or the oldest male, is the primary authority figure in the household and has the final say on all matters concerning the family. He is often a protective and highly respected figure in the family. Other male family members may make decisions for the rest of the group as well, and they are also given much respect and obedience. Even male children are given higher status than female children; sometimes girls are neglected by the family while boys are pampered.

The Case for Caste

A Dalit protests the caste system.

Patriarchy is not the only system of rank in Indian culture. Families are also designated as belonging to one of four groups, called *varnas*, which are classifications of people based on birth. This is known as the caste system, which can be understood as a sort of class structure of society. Members of different groups can and do associate with one another freely. However, caste members are expected to marry within their group and to adhere to the rules of behavior, diet, and other aspects of life appropriate to their class.

Rooted in Hinduism, this system of social organization dictates a set of values, social roles, and behaviors that is appropriate to the caste to which one belongs. The highest of the caste system are the Brahmans, also called priests, though not every member of this caste literally becomes a priest. Similarly, those in the next highest group, Ksatriyas, are not necessarily warriors, though this is what the name means. The next group is the Vaishyas. These people were initially peasants, but later evolved into the merchant class. The lowest of the four groups are the Shudras, who are serfs, or servants.

There is, however, one more class not commonly considered to be a true part of the caste system, but rather inferior to the four varnas. The Dalits, commonly referred to as "untouchables," are extremely poor and perform the most menial tasks of society, such as cleaning the public streets. They are called untouchables because they are thought to be polluted by the work they do. Although the caste system in India is technically illegal, it is often still a part of life—and a harsh part of life for this fifth, or outsider, caste. Dalits throughout India have been organizing and mobilizing their communities toward greater opportunities and social equality.

Teens typically have great respect for their grandmothers and all elders in the family and community.

The eldest female, or the wife of the patriarch, usually enjoys the highest status of all the female members of the family. She is responsible for delegating household duties to the other women and for seeing that all runs smoothly among them. The rest of the women are given due respect in order of their age and the number of sons they have. The behavior expected of women is different from that of men, although it does vary, depending on the area of India where one lives.

Family life prepares teens for the expectations of society, and teens basically respect and obey their elders. Parents often make decisions for teens as they grow up, mainly in the areas of education, career, and marriage.

Of course, teens in India, like those anywhere else, express their individuality and sometimes run into trouble with their parents for disobeying rules. For example, because teen dating is commonly frowned upon throughout India, teens who choose to date are likely to face punishment if caught.

The Activities of the Home

A common feature of an Indian home is a prayer room. While prayer rooms are predominantly found in Hindu homes, followers of other religions sometimes prepare such rooms as well.

Prayer rooms stimulate the senses with their decor and other details. The scent of incense, which is commonly used in Hindu worship rites, often fills the room. The walls may be decorated with elaborate, vibrant paintings of deities—perhaps ones with several arms, an elephant head, or green or blue skin. Statues often line shelves, along with framed pictures of holy figures and family members who have died. Prayer rooms are normally well-kept, though ash from the ever-present incense may be spilled here and there.

During the daily prayer time, family members repeat chanted prayers known as mantras. These prayers almost sound like songs, with their low, melodic tones.

During daily prayers, a lamp is often lit. This light symbolizes knowledge.

In homes where there is not enough space for a dedicated prayer room, religious items find a permanent place, and it is here that every member of the family comes to perform religious rituals and say prayers. Religious practices and beliefs of many faiths form an important part of the life of an Indian teen. Whether observed in the home or in public, these traditions are part of the moral, ethical, and social fabric of Indian culture.

Many of the rituals performed at home emphasize family ties. One ritual symbolizes the strong bonds between siblings. It takes place in the home when a brother touches the feet of his sister. This ritual is intended to show respect for the divinity of the female. Those who practice this ritual believe it will bring good fortune to the brother and the rest of the family. In both the northern and southern areas, sisters also bless their brothers to symbolically ask for protection from them in the future.

The home is not just about rules, rituals, and learning from elders; it is also a place to bring friends for fun in the evenings or on weekends. Indian teens have lots of friends, just like they have lots of family! Teens enjoy having sleepovers at their friends' houses or just hanging out in their bedrooms, listening to Hindi or Western music, dancing, and chatting.

Others Who Share the Home

Many middle- and upper-class families employ servants who do the majority of the housework. In India, it is common for a family to have a housemaid who sometimes also does the cooking and

The close relationships between brothers and sisters is celebrated with a festival, Raksha Bandhan. Sisters buy their brothers *rakhi* (sacred thread) to symbolically strengthen their bond.

helps with the children. Other families, mainly in the upper class, may employ several domestic servants to tend to each duty separately. These services are inexpensive in the city, and even lower-middle-class families may employ a housemaid or cook for about 300 to 800 rupees (U.S.$6 to $18) per month. Wealthier families may also employ a gardener to tend to their landscaping and even a security guard to protect their home.

Teen girls enjoy lighting oil lamps on the eve of the Hindu festival Diwali, known as the festival of lights.

CHAPTER FOUR

4 Every Day's a Holiday

FROM SNAKE-BOAT RACES TO CAMEL FAIRS, there is always something to look forward to in India, where every day is a holiday ... or, almost every day. One day you might see a crowd of people coming down the street singing and dancing, followed by a loud marching band. The next day there could be a parade full of colorful floats and dressed-up elephants. Most of the population take part in these celebrations.

The majority of the honored days have ties to religions. While Hindus make up the majority of the population, other religions have left their mark on Indian culture. These include Islam, Christianity,

Did You Know?

Dates for festivals change every year, following the Indian lunar calendar, which is based on the cycles of the moon. The lunar calendar is used by the government, but some people in India use the Islamic lunar calendar. Islam's calendar is about 11 days ahead of the Gregorian calendar, which is the calendar used most commonly around the world.

The 12 months of the Indian lunar calendar, also called the Hindu calendar, are between 30 and 31 days each. The actual dates that mark the beginning of the months may change each year.

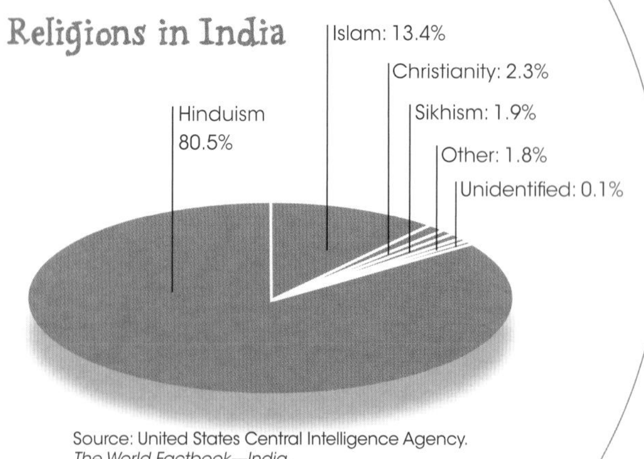

Source: United States Central Intelligence Agency. *The World Factbook—India.*

Buddhism, and lesser-known tribal religions. In fact, India has often been called a melting pot of religions, because each religion adds to the common culture of the whole. As a result, the calendar is packed with all sorts of holidays, festivals, celebrations, and special events.

National Holidays

Indians celebrate three national holidays. Independence Day, on August 15, is celebrated in honor of the day that India won its freedom after centuries of living under British rule.

Even though India gained independence in 1947, it wasn't until January 26, 1950, that the constitution

Schoolgirls march in Kolkata's Republic Day parade. Performances of traditional music and dances are also often part of the holiday's celebrations.

Ganesh's Festival

Ganesh Chaturthi is a special festival honoring Ganesh, the elephant-headed god of good fortune and clearer of obstacles—and one of the most loved and worshipped of the minor Hindu deities. Full-bodied and jolly, Ganesh is the god many Hindus pray to before beginning any new endeavor, from starting a new job to finding a suitable marriage partner. Most often pictured riding a ratlike creature and holding one broken tusk, Ganesh adorns many items, including calendars, T-shirts, and wedding invitations. During his festival, statues bearing his likeness are made, decorated, and elaborately dressed for a joyous parade through the busy city streets. Then they are lovingly released to float out to the sea.

During the festival, Ganesh is submerged in the Arabian Sea near Mumbai.

of India was put into practice. That day, known as Republic Day, is also honored. On Republic Day, stores and schools close and people enjoy the public holiday.

A large, fanciful parade is held in New Delhi, the capital of India, with members of the army, navy, and air force marching in full uniform. Following the military are many large and colorful floats. They make their way from the president's palace to India Gate, a large monument built to honor the Indian soldiers who died in World War I and the Afghan Wars (a series of wars between the United Kingdom and Afghanistan in the 19th and early 20th centuries).

The third national holiday is Gandhi Jayanti on October 2, the birthday of Mohandas Gandhi. Gandhi is known as the "father of the nation" for his crucial role in mobilizing millions of his fellow citizens to rid India of British rule. This holiday includes prayer services and tributes to Raj Ghat, Gandhi's memorial in New Delhi. Some schools and other organizations host essay contests in honor of Gandhi for this holiday. Prizes ranging from computers and digital cameras to publication in local newspapers and magazines.

Religious Celebrations & Festivals

Indians of all ages look forward to Diwali, the Hindu festival of lights. Depending on the area where it is celebrated, Diwali honors various

Rangoli are especially colorful for Diwali.

A Tasty Treat

Food is an important part of any Indian festival, and young and old love all the special treats. One popular treat is *kheer*, a type of pudding. Its base is made from milk combined with rice, vermicelli, coconut, or a number of other ingredients. Nuts, such as almonds or pistachios, or dried or fresh fruit are mixed in to make the dessert extra tasty. Cardamom, a spice commonly grown in India, is also often added. In fact, there are so many kinds of kheer, it would be difficult to choose a favorite!

kheer
kheer

Kheer is served at a number of Hindu and Islamic feasts and celebrations, including weddings. In the south. A version is presented to the gods in Hindu temples during special rituals.

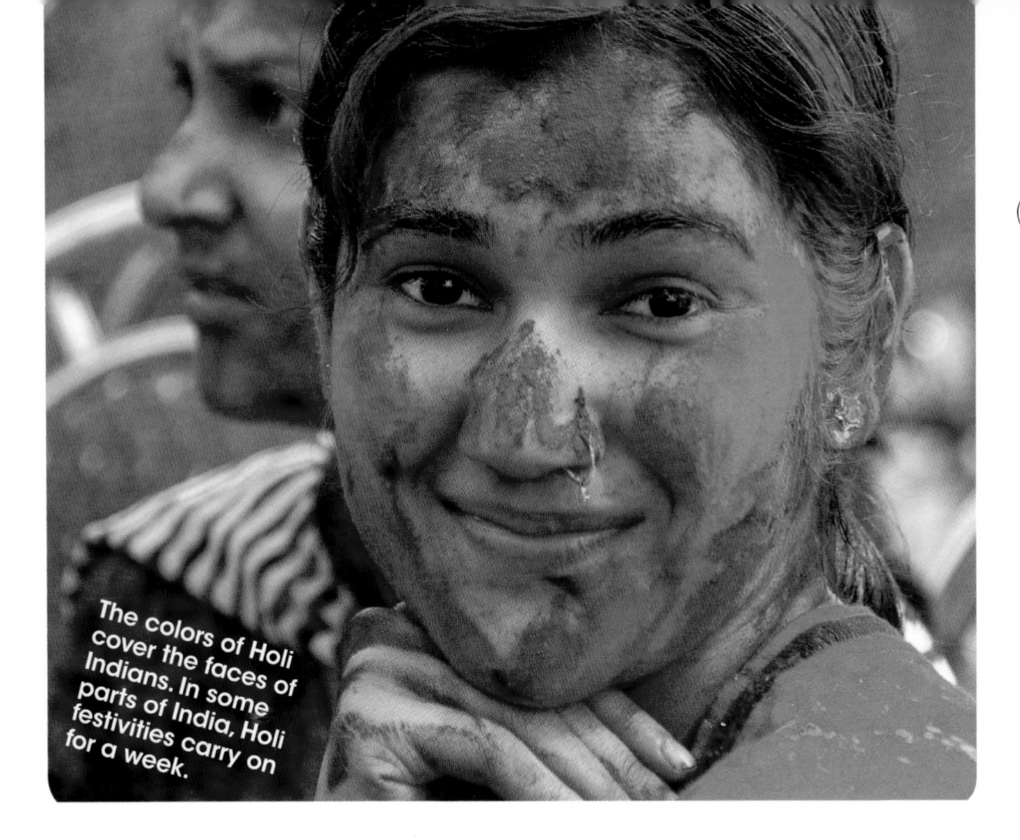
The colors of Holi cover the faces of Indians. In some parts of India, Holi festivities carry on for a week.

gods or goddesses. In general, though, it is seen as a celebration of good over evil.The celebration is very much like Christmas in other parts of the world, with greeting cards, special treats, and gifts. Many special dishes are prepared during this exciting holiday, and teen girls often help their mothers and aunts in the preparations.

During Diwali, people decorate their houses with beautiful chalk designs, and oil lamps are lit all over towns and villages for five days. Teens look forward to this festival all year for the extravagant displays of fireworks that light up the night sky. They enjoy indulging in holiday treats made of almonds, honey, and rice. For the most part, the holiday is a time for families to celebrate together, but many teens enjoy attending the public celebrations with groups of friends before joining their families later in the day.

Holi, the festival of colors, is another important festival in India. It is a great time for everyone, especially children and teenagers. Holi is a noisy, fun festival to celebrate the end of winter. Sometimes men and boys dress up in women's clothes, and many people play tricks on each other.

Out in the streets, people throw pink, blue, and silver paint or powder at each other, and the streets and sidewalks get very messy and colorful. Some say

At a Hindu wedding, a rope connects the couple and symbolizes their union.

the colors are used to show that special someone that he or she is loved, and teens look forward to this holiday so they can express their feelings to their special friends. Holi is also celebrated to honor a variety of religious legends and gods.

Samskara: Life Cycle Rituals

Special times in a person's life, such as marriage and childbirth, are celebrated with religious ceremonies and rituals. They vary depending on the area in which a person lives and the faith that person practices. Rituals known as *samskara*, or rite of passage, are most common among the Hindu population and are very important to the culture. Muslims throughout India also mark special occasions with religious ceremonies and large public functions.

samskara
SUM-skar-ah

Love & Marriage

If you see a Hindu priest tying the clothing of a bride and groom together, don't think that he is just fixing their clothes for pictures! He is actually "tying the knot" and joining the man and woman as husband and wife.

The journey to the *mandapa*, or wedding canopy, begins with the engagement. Most parents arrange marriages for their children. Sometimes families observe very strict arranged-marriage practices, in which a daughter or son has very little say in the matter of a partner. More often, however, arranged marriage refers to a system of arranged meetings—a type of blind date. Parents chose a suitable partner for their child, and the couple meet. If either party decides the union is not right, most families listen and other candidates are found.

Times are changing, and it is becoming more common for young men and women to choose their own partners. Either way, marriage is an important event to the whole family. Marriages in India bring together not only the happy couple but also their families and sometimes their villages or communities.

Once two families have agreed to a marriage, the families gather with grandparents, aunts, uncles, and close friends. The two families look at astrology charts to choose the best and luckiest day for the wedding. Sometimes gifts of jewelry are given to the bride by members of the groom's family. One custom involves a coconut, which is a sacred fruit in many parts of India. When the bride's parents give a coconut to the groom, the engagement is official.

Other traditions are performed by the groom's family. Sometimes they will give a new, beautiful sari to the bride and offer tasty treats to the bride's family. These traditions help

A three-month home-economics course in Bhopal is especially popular with engaged young women.

The mehndi designs are often applied by professional artists.

break the ice between the two families and between the bride and groom.

A day or two before the wedding, a party is held for the bride and her female friends, family, and future in-laws. At this party, the bride's hands and sometimes her feet are decorated with beautiful *mehndi* designs—painted with a paste made from the henna plant that stains the skin. Sometimes other women join in on the fun and have henna put on their hands, too, but their designs are never as beautiful as the bride's. These henna designs stay on the skin for a minimum of two weeks. Some say that others can tell how well a new bride is treated by how long her wedding henna lasts.

The wedding ceremonies themselves vary from area to area and among faiths. There are some similarities, however. Wedding decorations tend to be very beautiful and colorful, and often many fresh flowers are used.

Most weddings involve as many friends and family members as possible. The bride's family is responsible for feeding and housing the guests because the wedding usually takes place in the bride's home. The party can last for several days after the wedding ceremony.

Seven Steps

Saptapadi, or "taking seven steps together," is an important wedding ritual performed in many Hindu weddings. The steps are taken by the bride and groom, sometimes around a fire or along a line of seven nuts. They represent the seven promises that the bride and groom make to each other and to their families and friends:

1. We will be caring and patient with one another.
2. We will stand together in sorrow and bliss.
3. We will be respectful, honest, and true with one another.
4. We will travel the journey of life with love and harmony.
5. We will raise moral and virtuous children.
6. We will do everything to keep our family happy, healthy, and strong.
7. We will search together for knowledge and beauty.

The bride and groom circle the fire three times to formalize their union.

The 2006 wedding of model Priya Sachdev and the son of a wealthy hotel owner, Vikram Chatwal, was considered one of India's most lavish celebrations in years.

baraat
bar-RAHT

One tradition that is common in north Indian weddings is for the groom to arrive on a white horse with his family and friends—and sometimes a band—following him. This is called the *baraat*, or wedding procession. Often the bride and groom welcome each other by exchanging flower garlands before they enter the mandapa to be married. The wedding ceremony is performed by a priest and is filled with sacred rituals, all of which are meant to give good luck and happiness to the new couple.

Pregnancy & Birth

Not long after the marriage, the newlyweds are expected to start a family. In some places, a woman wears a yellow veil with a large red spot to tell everyone that she is pregnant. There are many rituals that may be performed during a pregnancy. Some women make offerings to Naga, the Hindu snake god of fertility. Some ceremonies are performed during pregnancy to ensure the health of the mother and child. One of these rituals is the parting of the mother's hair three times by the baby's father.

The birth of a baby is often celebrated with songs, sweets, and gifts.

When a boy is born, there is a great celebration that may involve blowing conch shells or beating drums.

In some areas, birth celebrations for baby girls are not as common or elaborate because boy children are generally preferred. In rural areas, male children will grow up to help with agricultural duties. In communities where large dowries are expected in order to find a suitable partner for a female child, a baby girl can mean a major expense later.

Visitors often express their sorrow for the new parents' "burden." A new father told a BBC News reporter about his family's experience following his daughter's birth:

"Relatives arrived laden with gifts of sweet meats. They cuddled her and shook their heads at our misfortune."

For these and other reasons, in some areas, when a girl is born, the women hide behind their veils and cry.

No matter the sex of the child, certain rituals are performed during childhood. At birth, the father may touch the baby's lips with gold, often a spoon or ring that is dipped in honey or a special kind of butter called ghee. Sometimes mantras will be said to wish the child a long, happy life. Other ceremonies include the reading of the child's first horoscope and the naming of the child. For both boys and girls, there is often an ear-piercing ceremony and another ceremony when the child first eats solid food, which is usually cooked rice.

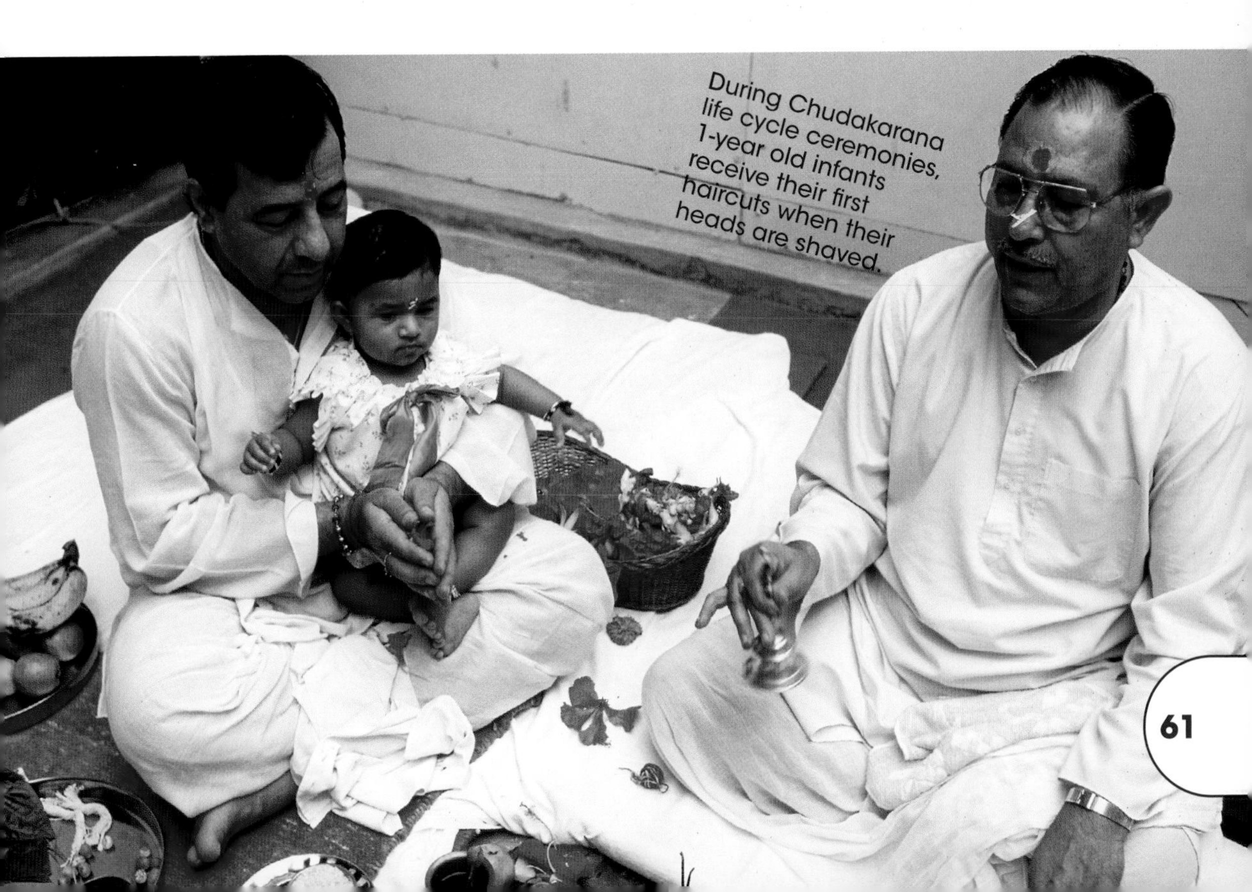

During Chudakarana life cycle ceremonies, 1-year old infants receive their first haircuts when their heads are shaved.

Despite a boom in the technology industries, the vast majority of Indians are manual laborers.

5

CHAPTER FIVE

Work in a Country of Change

BY 6 A.M. THE STREETS OF CITIES THROUGHOUT INDIA ARE BUSTLING WITH ACTIVITY. Young professionals dressed in white linen shirts and dark trousers hurry past on their way to the office. Meanwhile *walla* prepare their goods for sale on the streets. Domestic servants dressed in plain cotton saris make their way through the already forming crowds. They take care of early morning errands on their way to the homes of their employers. Groups of young men and women cross the street together, avoiding those who zip by on motor scooters to their jobs in other parts of the city.

While children and teens walk or catch buses to school, the rest of the city prepares for the busy

What's a Walla?

Those who set up shop to sell specific items—sometimes on the side of the road, sometimes in more permanent structures—are called walla, the Hindi word for "seller." The number and type of walla in India are beyond count—in one day, you could pass a padlock walla, a paan walla, a rug walla, a bicycle walla, a vest walla, and on and on.

The small fingers of underage workers are favored by garment manufacturers who specialize in clothing with crystal embellishments.

day ahead. Miles away in the country villages, teens and adults alike are heading out to the fields to tend the crops. Elderly women and teen girls stay behind to tidy up the house and begin preparation for the midday meal. India is alive with activity as the people in

both the city and country begin their day's work.

Young Workers & Their Labor

It is uncommon for teenagers in India to have part-time jobs after school. Cultural tradition dictates that people do not begin working outside the home until they are 21 years old. Some teens and young children, however, find sources of work to contribute to their families' incomes.

For teens living in poverty, both in the city and the country, work takes precedence over study and leisure time. In large cities like New Delhi, some teens take on jobs such as washing cars and pushing handcarts. Although the employment of children in factories is against the law, it is not uncommon for children as young as 4 years old to be found working in factories, making glass bangle bracelets, matches, and other common products.

In the area of Tamil Nadu, an estimated 45,000 children and teens work in industries manufacturing matches, fireworks, and printing products. These teens work long hours every day and find little time for leisure activities.

In rural areas, teens are often required to labor alongside the family in agricultural work. Sometimes these teens only go to school until they are 14 years old and then work with the family full time.

Many teens in the lower classes also work as servants in the homes of families of the higher classes to earn money for the family. Some find it necessary to dig through piles of garbage to find food items, sources of fuel, and other items that might be sold for profit.

Indian Industry

Historically, much of the employment of India revolved around agriculture. As cities have become more populous and new industries more common, more Indians than ever are working away from the home and the farms. While India's main export items still include many agricultural products, the country competes in the global market with many other industries, including the manufacture of textiles and handicrafts.

The rise of the information technology (IT) industry in India has had a significant impact on the economy, as well as on the lives of residents. They are able to find secure and well-paying jobs in this growing, modern market. In addition, jobs in the telecommunication industry, banking, and manufacturing are plentiful in India.

Harvested grain is carried in a large basket on top of the head.

Common Crops

Common Crops
Rice
Sugar
Bananas
Mangoes
Coconuts
Cashews
Potatoes
Tomatoes
Citrus fruits
Pineapples

Roots in Agriculture

Despite these new industries, 65 percent of the labor force is still employed in agricultural pursuits. Although agricultural products only make up about 26 percent of the gross domestic product, India is still a world leader in the production of foods, such as potatoes, okra, peas, milk, wheat, rice, sugar, and fruit. Agricultural work can be a demanding and time-consuming job, not to mention tiring. But farmers and their teenage helpers take pride in their work.

The state of Punjab is often called the "breadbasket of India" or the "granary of

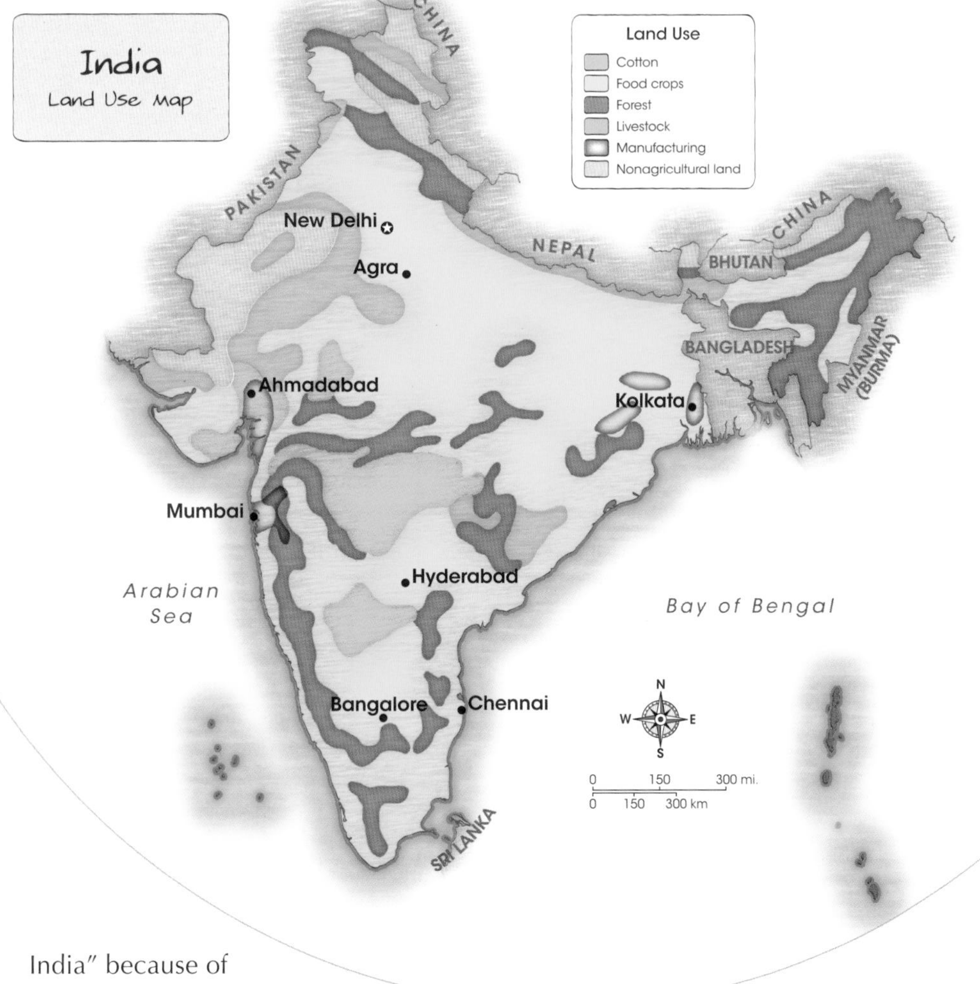

India" because of its large production of wheat and rice. The state is one of the nation's foremost producers of agricultural products, with around 85 percent of its land covered in fields. Although there are urban areas in Punjab, the majority of teens living in this area are quite knowledgeable about agriculture and spend a great deal of their time working alongside their families, especially during harvest time.

Textiles & IT

India is also well-known for its manufacture of machinery and chemicals. By far the biggest industry is textiles, employing more than 90 million people throughout the country. The textile industry is important to the country because it provides one of the basic necessities of life, employs so many, and generates export earnings.

Got Bling?

Jewelry is an important part of fashion in India, and many Indians play important roles in the manufacture and distribution of fine jewelry for trade with other countries. Many women wear lots of bangles—thin bracelets made of gold, silver, or white metal. Rings, necklaces, and earrings are signs of wealth and status in the culture. Gold is in high demand and is very expensive. Many semiprecious stones and gems are mined in various parts of India as well, and the country is the world leader in the cut and polished diamond market.

Throughout history, and especially during the Mughal Empire in the 15th to 17th centuries, precious stones were used not only as ornamentation for women but also in the decoration of buildings and household items. The Taj Mahal, a white marble shrine in Agra, is an example of this type of extravagant decoration.

Many Indian call centers provide service to international customers.

There are numerous options for those seeking work in the textile industry, including the manufacture of fabrics such as sari material and ornate drapery.

Most teen girls learn fancy needlework and appliqué at home or at school while they are still young. Those who enjoy it or are especially talented may choose to pursue a career in creating beautiful clothing, rugs, bedding, and other detailed items. Although teens do not usually take jobs outside the home before their schooling is complete, some teen girls produce finely crafted articles of clothing and bedding for sale in local shops to supplement the family income.

India has a long history of supplying the trade market with these beautifully crafted textiles. In today's market, both in India and abroad, lavishly decorated items such as saris and shawls are much admired. Large factories all over India employ millions of skilled crafts-people in this important industry.

The information technology industry has grown to be a major contender in the employment field in India. Jobs in IT, software, and other related areas are extremely popular among the up-and-coming generation. Parents of teens may particularly want their children to pursue these careers. Many colleges in India are specialized to train students in this competitive field, and these institutions have prepared a large resource of highly skilled workers.

Going off to College

India has more than 180 universities, around 500 teacher-training colleges, and several thousand other colleges that cater to specific careers such as engineering and information technology. In the past, higher education was a privilege of only the wealthy upper class. In recent years, however, higher education has become increasingly available to any student graduating from high school. In the early 1950s, college and university enrollment was only about 360,000. In the 1990s, enrollment reached nearly 4 million.

Admission to non-professional colleges is not terribly competitive. In contrast, without the highest of high school grades, it can be extremely difficult to get into professional colleges in certain fields. Architecture, business, medicine, and dentistry are highly profitable and therefore popular.

The Janpath Handicraft Market in New Delhi provides a selling location for handicrafters.

Many cities in India have encouraged the influx of the IT industry. The most renowned, the southern city of Bangalore, is often called India's Silicon Valley. It is in reference to an area in northern California where many technology-based companies are located.

Finding a Job

Even with the abundant opportunities for employment, the large population of India makes securing a well-paying job difficult in many areas. Often it is necessary to seek the help of relatives and friends in order to find employment in large cities. Those without a good network of people to help them face great challenges.

There is an array of opportunities

for Indians outside the major industries. People may find jobs in construction, restaurants, or retail—selling a remarkable assortment of goods, from prepared foods to beautiful handicrafts.

Throughout India, as in much of the world, women of poor and lower-class communities have always worked outside the home. Since the 1980s, middle- and upper-class women have broken many boundaries and joined the paid work force in record numbers. As in other parts of the world, women still face much gender discrimination in employment, however, and are often paid less than men for the same work.

One excuse for this difference in pay is commonly given in the construction industry. Women often need to take short breaks to tend to their children—especially if they have young ones who are still breast-feeding. Employers lower their wages to account for the missed time, even though that time could be made up.

Many employers consider women less deserving of equal wages since they are commonly considered to be physically weaker. Women all over the world challenge these barriers by organizing for social change. Groups such as the Self-Employed Women's Association (SEWA) in Ahmedabad are working hard to improve the employment opportunities and conditions for women in large cities.

Women's activist Ela Bhatt is the head of SEWA.

A common pastime among teens is cricket, India's most popular sport.

6

CHAPTER SIX

From Cricket to Bollywood

TEENS THROUGHOUT INDIA EMBRACE THEIR LEISURE TIME. In rural areas, sports and the great outdoors provide an escape from the hard work of the day. Bike riding with friends is a fun pastime for teens, and rural teen boys are considered cool if they have their own bike.

In cities, teens can see movies, go shopping, or simply watch the action of street performers, tourists, and sometimes animals around them. The city's activity can make getting around extremely difficult. Traffic is chaotic because of the large number of vehicles driving in unmarked lanes and the crowds of people on the streets.

Age Old Entertainment

Catching a puppet show on the streets of cities like New Delhi or Mumbai is a favorite pastime for many teens. Puppetry in India is an old profession, and though the popularity of this form of theater has decreased in recent years, puppeteers can still be found in many areas around the country. The puppeteer, who is always male, uses detailed wooden puppets in bright, extravagant costumes to tell stories from the epic histories of India and religious mythology. Although teens commonly prefer television and movies to puppet shows, many still make their way to the shows for a fun outing in the city.

Throughout India, shopping is growing in popularity with the middle and upper classes. In recent years, retail sales have risen 28 percent per year.

Road accidents are the leading cause of accidental death—estimated to be 20 times as high as in other countries with high automobile traffic. This is partly caused by poorly planned roads and lane divisions. Many city dwellers do not like to hassle with driving, so upper-class families often employ a full-time driver.

Since the age for getting a driver's license is 18, most teens do not have to worry about fighting the traffic to get around town in a car. Instead, they may depend on a bike or they may simply stroll the city streets to get where they need to go, take in the sights, or window shop.

What to Do? City Highlights

For those who have some money to spend, there are several attractions in cities that make a night out or a day on the town a good time. Nightclubs are common in large cities. There are a few that are independently operated, but most are found in upscale hotels.

While older teens might enjoy an occasional night out at one of these hotspots, they are generally very expensive places to visit. Frequently the clubs require a large "door charge," a fee just to enter. Inside, the drinks and food are often outrageously priced. Most hotels restrict entrance to members and hotel guests, so most

Fun Film Facts

India produces more films annually than any other country. More than 800 films are produced every year! The Indian film industry is nicknamed "Bollywood," a take off on Hollywood. It is based in the large city of Mumbai. Most of the movies that come out of Bollywood are commercial Hindi films, but films in other languages are also very common. The best known filmmaker from India is Satyajit Ray, who made many successful films in the Bengali language. After his death in 1992, he was honored with the prestigious Academy Award for lifetime achievement.

Girls of all backgrounds enjoy playing hockey.

Bollywood stars Shah Rukh Kan and Shilpa Shetty

residents prefer to entertain at home with their family and friends.

Significantly less expensive, and more common, is the cinema, or movie theater. Almost every town in India has a cinema, and the ticket prices are generally very low. Tickets range in price from 20 to 150 rupees (U.S. 45 cents to $3).

Teens love going to the cinema with their friends. Seeing a movie in India is not an occasion for hushed voices and silent viewing. It can be a raucous party with everyone clapping and cheering.

Another fun outing enjoyed by teens and adults alike is a sporting event. Although the national sport of India is hockey, which has a large number of fans, soccer matches are even more popular in some areas, particularly in the northeast. For those who enjoy watching tennis, large urban centers offer matches. Although ticket prices are generally a bit higher, they are still affordable for an occasional outing. Among the upper class, polo is a popular sport, and families often attend daylong matches together.

Cricket is by far the most popular sport in India to both watch and play. It is similar to baseball, with innings played by teams alternating batting and fielding. However the field and techniques are slightly different. Cricket is played between teams of 11 players each, and games can last from a few hours to a few days. All over India, cricket is played by young children, teens, and adults for fun and exercise. Many schools have cricket teams, and often neighborhood friends and relatives organize games for a fun weekend or evening activity.

International cricket matches, held mainly during the winter, can be seen in several major cities in India, including Mumbai and Bangalore. Fans cheer wildly for the home team as they play against countries such as England, Pakistan, and Australia. These games can sometimes continue over several days. Ticket prices vary from relatively inexpensive seats for 200 to 400 rupees (U.S.$4.50 to $9) to first-rate seats that may cost up to 1,000 rupees (U.S.$22), with tea and lunch included. With the wide range of ticket prices and seats available, cricket matches are fun outings most Indian teens can occasionally experience.

Cricket tends to be played anywhere—from the streets to the beach.

Beyond the City

India is a thriving mix of bustling big cities and hardworking rural villages. Approximately half a million villages are scattered all over India. Most villages have fewer than 1,000 residents. Many urban residents speak fondly of village life, suggesting that it is a simpler,

peaceful existence. They may be drawn to visit friends and family in the countryside as an escape from the commotion and hassle of city life.

The images of village life—with stretches of uninterrupted fields filled with cattle and a variety of birds, and people coming and going with water pots on their heads—suggest an almost ideal location for relaxation. Ideal, that is, if one is visiting and not expected to contribute to the hard work that leaves little time for rural folk to relax and play.

A popular activity for both locals and tourists is the safari. India has 88 national parks and 490 wildlife

Walking the Sacred Path

In India, pilgrimages are known as *yatra*. Devout Hindus are expected to make these journeys regularly, at least once a year if possible. Most often people make pilgrimages to aid in their spiritual development, to pray to God in holy places, and, in the case of Hindus, to honor the many deities that are a part of God.

There are many other reasons to make such a trip. Sometimes people make pilgrimages to pray for certain things, to ask for blessings, or to heal physically or emotionally. Others do so to take the ashes of deceased loved ones to a final resting place at a sacred site.

yatra
YAHTH-rah

Varanasi is a holy city to which devout Hindus hope to travel at least once in their lives. Other such cities include Dwarka, Ayodhya, and Mathura. There are also seven rivers in India that are considered to be sacred. The most frequently visited are the Ganges and Indus rivers. Other sacred places may be found in the mountains and countrysides, in places like caves, and at other natural landforms that are associated with the historical epics of India.

The Amarnath cave shrine is a pilgrimage destination for more than 500,000 Hindus annually.

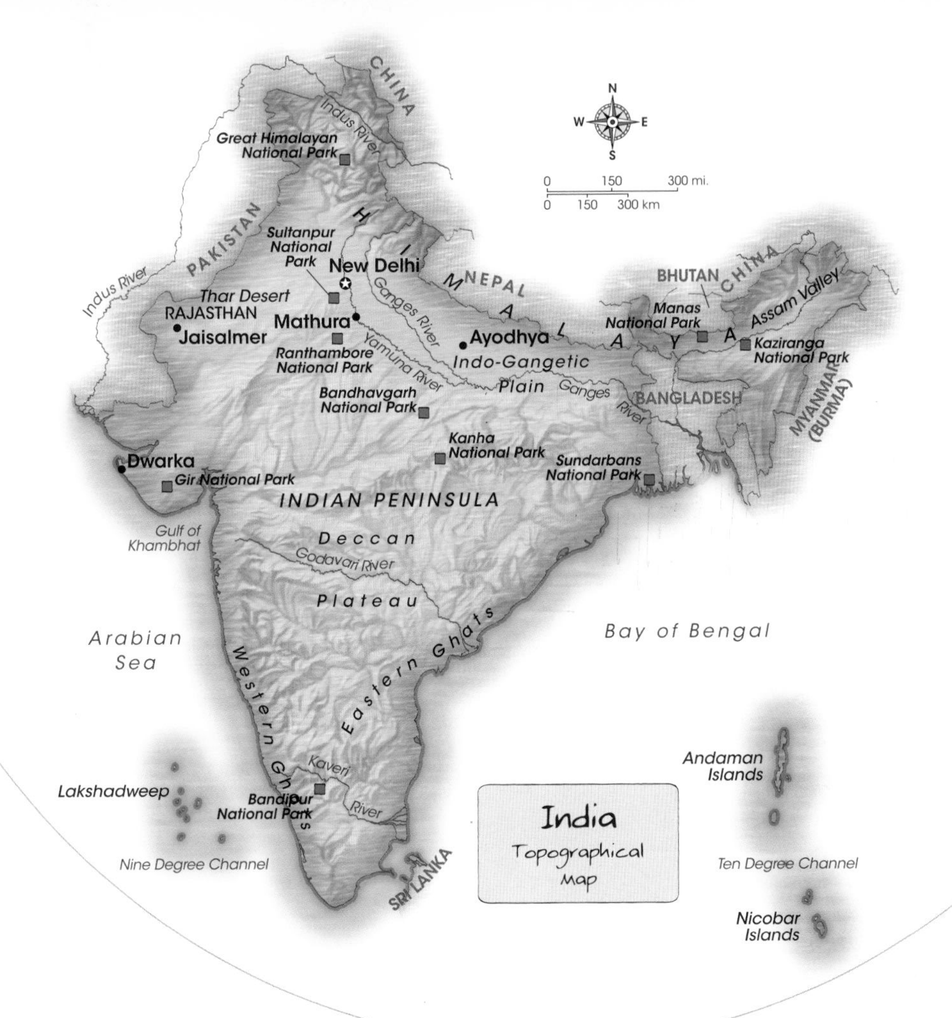

sanctuaries. All kinds of beautiful animals may be spotted during a jungle safari: herds of elephants, peacocks, bison, a variety of deer, and, if you are lucky, even the majestic Bengal tiger.

Teens do not travel on safari on their own; they are normally on family vacations. The mode of transportation can create a unique safari experience. Camel safaris are offered at a park near Jaisalmer, and safari on horseback is offered in Rajasthan. Or families may choose to visit one of the many parks that offer jeep safaris.

There is a wide range of things to do at a safari camp, and new activities are being added all the time. A new private forest reserve in Shivalik, for example, offers off-road biking. The safari adventures, lasting from a few hours to a few days, are wonderful ways for families to relax together and to explore nature.

Looking Ahead

INDIA IS THE SEVENTH-LARGEST COUNTRY IN THE WORLD, with the second-largest population, estimated at more than 1 billion. Only China has more people. Despite the overcrowding and poverty that go along with this huge population, teens live inspiring and meaningful lives filled with many interesting pastimes and endeavors.

Because India is one of the most diverse assemblies of people, religions, and traditions in the world, it is difficult to make generalizations about the culture of India or the experiences of the teens who call India home. But one thing is certain: Teens are looking forward to a better future for themselves, their families, and their country. As changes take place in the economy of India, more opportunities for successful careers make the outlook seem brighter for teens who are willing to work hard to achieve their dreams.

At a Glance

Official name: Republic of India

Capital: New Delhi

People

Population: 1,095,351,995

Population by age groups:
0–14 years: 30.8%
15–64 years: 64.3%
65 years and up: 4.9%

Life expectancy at birth: 64.71 years

Official languages: Hindi (national language), English, Bengali, Telugu, Marathi, Tamil, Urdu, Gujarati, Malayalam, Kannada, Oriya, Punjabi, Assamese, Kashmiri, Sindhi, Sanskrit

Religions:
Hinduism: 80.5%
Islam: 13.4%
Christianity: 2.3%
Sikhism: 1.9%
Other: 1.8%
Unidentified: 0.1%

Legal ages:
Alcohol consumption: Varies by state
Driver's license: 18
Employment: 14
Marriage: 18 (female), 21 (male)
Military service: 16
Voting: 18

Government

Type of government: Federal republic

Chief of state: President, elected by an electoral college consisting of members of Sansad (Parliament) and state legislatures

Head of government: Prime minister, chosen by parliamentary members of the majority party

Lawmaking body: Sansad (Parliament); consists of the Rajya Sabha (Council of State) and Lok Sabha (the People's Assembly)

Administrative divisions: 28 states and seven union territories

Independence: August 15, 1947 (from the United Kingdom)

National holiday: Republic Day, January 26, 1950

National symbols:
Animal: Royal Bengal tiger
Bird: Peacock
Flower: Lotus
Tree: Banyan
Fruit: Mango
Sport: Hockey

Geography

Total area: 1,315,036 square miles (3,287,590 square kilometers)

Climate: Varies from tropical in the south to temperate in the north. Winter (November to March) is bright and pleasant with snowfall in the northern hills. Summer (April to June) is hot and dry. A monsoon season produces heavy

rainfall along the west coast from June through September and along the east coast from October through December.

Highest point: Kanchenjunga, 28,373 feet (8,598 meters)

Lowest point: Indian Ocean, sea level

Major landforms: Indo-Gangetic Plain, Himalaya mountain range, Indian Peninsula, Thar Desert, Assam Valley, Islands of the Arabian Sea

Major rivers: Ganges, Godavari, Indus, Kaveri, Yamuna

Economy

Currency: Indian rupee

Population below poverty line: 25%

Major natural resources: Coal, iron ore, manganese, mica, bauxite, titanium ore, chromite, natural gas, diamonds, petroleum, limestone

Major agricultural products: Rice, wheat, oilseed, cotton, jute, tea, sugarcane, potatoes, cattle, water buffalo, sheep, goats, poultry, fish

Major exports: Textile goods, gems and jewelry, engineering goods, chemicals, leather products

Major imports: Crude oil, machinery, gems, fertilizer, chemicals

Historical Timeline

2000 B.C. — Bronze Age well established in Europe

1500-500 B.C. — During the Aryan Empire, the caste system of societal hierarchy develops

321-184 B.C. — The Mauryan Empire controls most of what is now India

A.D. 250 — The Maya rise to prominence in Central America

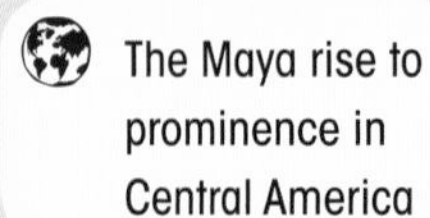

1175 — Muslim ruler Muhammed of Ghur begins a campaign to conquer India

1600s — British colonies are established in North America

1780s — The British East India Company controls much of the country

1799 — Napoléon Bonaparte seizes power in France

Historical World Event

1846

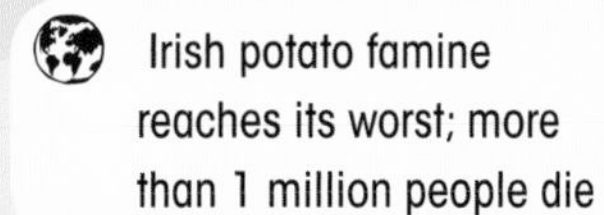
Irish potato famine reaches its worst; more than 1 million people die

1858

The Indian Mutiny is unsuccessful, and India is officially under the rule of the British Crown

1914-1918

World War I

1920

Mohandas Gandhi (1869–1948) begins to lead the country in nonviolent protests against English colonial rule

1939-1945

World War II

1947

Independence is gained on August 15, but the country is divided into mainly Hindu India and Muslim-majority Pakistan

1966

Indira Gandhi becomes India's first female prime minister and serves until 1977; serves again from 1980 until her assassination in 1989

1969

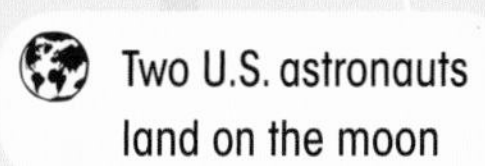
Two U.S. astronauts land on the moon

Historical Timeline

1989

 The Berlin Wall falls

1991

Prime Minister P.V. Narasimha Rao begins an economic-reform program

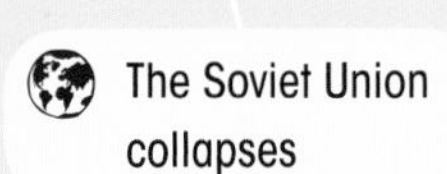

The Soviet Union collapses

2000

In May, India's billionth citizen is born

2001

 Terrorist attacks on the two World Trade Center towers in New York City and on the Pentagon in Washington, D.C., leave thousands dead

2004

More than 10,700 Indians are killed by a powerful tsunami; coastal communities in the south and the Andaman and Nicobar Islands are especially devastated

2006

The government launches a rural-jobs program designed to bring 60 million families out of poverty

Pluto is demoted to dwarf planet status more than 70 years after its discovery

Glossary

dialects	forms of a language that are spoken in particular areas or by particular groups of people
dowries	money or property given to the groom's family by the bride's at the time of marriage
Gregorian calendar	the calendar used by much of the world; it was established in 1582 by Pope Gregory XIII
gross domestic product	the total value of all goods and services produced in a country during a specific period
hierarchy	the classification of a group of people according to ability or to economic, social, or professional standing
incarnations	the embodiment of a deity or spirit in earthly forms
literacy	the quality or state of being able to read
menial	of or relating to servants; lowly; lacking dignity
nuclear family	family group that consists only of a father, mother, and children
ornate	elaborately or excessively decorated
patriarchal	having to do with the father being in charge of the family
pilgrimage	journey to a holy place
prominent	widely and popularly known; leading
raucous	noisy and disorderly
threshing	separating seed from a harvested plant

Additional Resources

IN THE LIBRARY

Ganeri, Anita. *Exploration into India.* New York: Chelsea House, 2000.

Heydlauff, Lisa, and Nitin Upadyhe. *Going to School in India.* Watertown, Mass.: Charlesbridge, 2005.

Kalman, Bobbie. *India: The Culture.* New York: Crabtree Publishing, 2000.

Malaspina, Ann. *Mahatma Gandhi and India's Independence in World History.* Berkeley Heights, N.J.: Enslow Publishers, 2000.

Schomp, Virginia. *Ancient India.* New York: Franklin Watts, 2005.

Swan, Erin Pembrey. *India.* New York: Children's Press, 2002.

ON THE WEB

For more information on this topic, use FactHound.

1. Go to www.facthound.com
2. Type in this book ID: 0756520630
3. Click on the *Fetch It* button.

Look for more Global Connections books.

Teens in Australia
Teens in Brazil
Teens in China
Teens in France
Teens in Israel
Teens in Japan
Teens in Kenya
Teens in Mexico
Teens in Russia
Teens in Saudi Arabia
Teens in Spain
Teens in Venezuela
Teens in Vietnam

Source Notes

Page 14, column 1, line 1: Sumita Kale. "Sumita Kale: Of Primary Importance." *Business Standard*. 12 July 2006. 12 July 2006. www.business-standard.com/ common/ storypage.php?autono=97951&leftnm=4&subLeft=0&chkFlg=

Page 18, line 27: Vineeta Pandey. "Too Many Schools Sans Blackboards." *Daily News & Analysis*. 10 July 2006. 12 July 2006. www.dnaindia.com/report.asp?NewsID=1040849

Page 26, column 1, line 1: Sarina Singh et al. *India*. Oakland, Calif.: Lonely Planet Publications, 2003, p. 57.

Page 30, column 1, line 6. Tharoor, Shashi. *India: From Midnight to the Millennium*. New York: Arcade Publishing, 1997, p. 56.

Page 61, column 1, line 19: Navdip Dhariwal. "The 'Curse' of Having a Girl." *BBC Delhi*. 29 June 2006. 12 July 2006. http://news.bbc.co.uk/2/hi/programmes/5125810.stm.

Pages 84–85, At a Glance: United States. Central Intelligence Agency. *The World Factbook: India*. 2005. 20 June 2005. www.cia.gov/cia/publications/factbook/geos/in.html

Select Bibliography

"At What Age?" The Right to Education Project. December 2005. 25 Jan. 2006. www.right-to-education.org/content/age/india.html

Babu, Uma Jagdesh. Personal interview. 18 Nov. 2005.

Dhariwal, Navdip. "The 'Curse' of Having a Girl." *BBC Delhi.* 29 June 2006. 12 July 2006. http://news.bbc.co.uk/2/hi/programmes/5125810.stm

"Divorce Rate in India." Divorce Rate.org. 14 May 2006. www.divorcerate.org/divorce-rate-in-india.html

Dunlop, Fiona. *Fodor's Exploring India.* New York: Fodor's Travel Publications, 2004.

Gesser, Veronica, and Rimjhim Banerjee. "India." *Teen Life in Asia.* Ed. Judith J. Slater. Westport, Conn.: Greenwood Press, 2004, pp. 51–67.

"India and Pakistan: Fifty Years of Independence." *CNN.com.* 1997. 25 Jan. 2005. www.cnn.com/WORLD/9708/India97/index.html

"Indian Calendar." Calendars Through the Ages. 22 Nov. 2005. http://webexhibits.org/calendars/calendar-indian.html

"India: Adult Illiteracy." U.N. Common Database. Globalis–India. 16 Nov. 2006. http://globalis.gvu.unu.edu/indicator_detail.cfm?Country=IN&IndicatorID=27#row

"India: Textile Sector is the 2nd Largest Employment Provider." *Fiber2Fashion.* 11 July 2006. 12 July 2006. www.fibre2fashion.com/news/textile-news/newsdetails.aspx?news_id=19685.

Jagga, Raakhi. "Night Safaris in New Forest Getaway." *Ludhiana Newsline*. 29 June 2006. 12 July 2006. http://cities.expressindia.com/ fullstory.php?newsid=190441

Kale, Sumita. "Sumita Kale: Of Primary Importance." *Business Standard*. 12 July 2006. 12 July 2006. www.business-standard.com/common/storypage.php?autono=97951&leftnm=4&subLeft=0&chkFlg=

Pandey, Vineeta. "Too Many Schools Sans Blackboards." *Daily News & Analysis*. 10 July 2006. 12 July 2006. www.dnaindia.com/report.asp?NewsID=1040849

Raeshma, Jacob. Personal interview. 7 Oct. 2005.

Republic of India. Ministry of Human Resource Development. 14 May 2006. http://education.nic.in/

Republic of India. Registrar General and Census Commissioner, India. *Census of India*. 16 May 2006. www.censusindia.net/

Sarkar, Saswati. Personal interview. 6 May 2006.

"Secondary School Curriculum 2005–2007." Central Board of Secondary Education. 16 Nov. 2006. http://cbse.nic.in/public1.htm

Singh, Sarina et al. *India*. Oakland, Calif.: Lonely Planet Publications, 2003.

Tharoor, Shashi. *India: From Midnight to the Millennium*. New York: Arcade Publishing, 1997.

"Timeline: India." *BBC News*. 11 July 2006. 16 Aug. 2006. http://news.bbc.co.uk/1/hi/world/south_asia/country_profiles/1155813.stm

United States. Central Intelligence Agency. *The World Factbook: India*. 2005. 20 June 2005. www.cia.gov/cia/publications/factbook/geos/in.html

United States. Library of Congress. Federal Research Division. *A Country Study: India*. Eds. James Heitzman and Robert L. Worden. Washington, D.C.: Government Printing Office, 1995.

Index

About the Author
Lori Shores

Lori Shores is a recent graduate of Minnesota State University, Mankato, with a master's degree in literature. She shares her home with her brilliant son, two crazy cats, a silly hamster, and one confused fish. When she is not busy writing and reading, she is planning future trips all over the world, including her new favorite country, India.

About the Content Adviser
Anu Taranath, Ph.D.

Dr. Anu Taranath is a senior lecturer in the Department of English at the University of Washington, Seattle. She is especially interested in colonial, postcolonial, feminist, and pedagogical issues. She serves as program director for a study-abroad program to Bangalore, India, entitled "Globalization and Social Justice."

Image Credits

Tauseef Mustafa/AFP/Getty Images, cover, 41 (bottom), 76–77; Kharidehal Abhirama/BigStockPhoto, back cover (top); Vera Bogaerts/Shutterstock, back cover (bottom); Corel, 1 (left); Dhoxax/Shutterstock, 1 (middle); Vishal Shah/Shutterstock, 1 (right), 5, 36 (top); Pei Lin Shang/BigStockPhoto, 2–3; Aravind Teki/Shutterstock, 4, 7 (right), 26, 90; Jin Young Lee/BigStockPhoto, 6 (top); Aravind Teki/BigStockPhoto, 6 (bottom); Sudheendra Kadri/BigStockPhoto, 7 (left); Hugh Sitton/zefa/Corbis, 8–9; Deshakalyan Chowdhury/AFP/Getty Images, 10; Thierry Falise/OnAsia, 12–13, 42; Prakash Singh/AFP/Getty Images, 14, 19, 22–23, 30, 64 (bottom); Robert Nickelsberg/Getty Images, 16–17; Sanjeev Gupta/epa/Corbis, 20; Raveendran/AFP/Getty Images, 21; Fernando Bengoechea/Beateworks/Corbis, 24; Robert Holmes/Corbis, 27; Anthony Cassidy/Stone/Getty Images, 28; Robert Harding Picture Library Ltd/Alamy, 29; World Religions Photo Library/Alamy, 31, 45; Cephas Picture Library/Alamy, 32; John MacDougall/AFP/Getty Images, 33; David Wells/Alamy, 34; William Albert Allard/Getty Images, 36 (bottom); Ng Yin Chern/Shutterstock, 37; Tibor Bognar/Alamy, 38; Ursula Dþren/dpa/Corbis, 40–41; Indranil Mukherjee/AFP/Getty Images, 43, 53; Dana Ward/Shutterstock, 44, 55, 66, 78–79; Narinder Nanu/AFP/Getty Images, 46–47; Amit Dave/Reuters/Corbis, 48; Reuters/Corbis, 50–51; Punit Paranjpe/Reuters/Corbis, 52, 76 (bottom); Food Features/Alamy, 54; Michel Setboun/Corbis, 56; STR/AFP/Getty Images, 57; Vincent Long/OnAsia, 58; Earl & Nazima Kowall/Corbis, 59; Manpreet Romana/AFP/Getty Images, 60; Lindsay Hebberd/Corbis, 61; Angus McDonald/OnAsia, 62, 64–65; iconex/Shutterstock, 68; Sherwin Crasto/Reuters/Corbis, 69; John Elk III, 70–71; Robert Nickelsberg/Time Life Pictures/Getty Images, 71 (bottom); David Sutherland/Corbis, 72; Free Agents Limited/Corbis, 74; Sanjit Das/OnAsia, 75; Altaf Qudri/epa/Corbis, 80; Ralf Hirschberger/dpa/Corbis, 82–83; Eromaze/Dreamstime, 84 (top); Steffen Foerster Photography/Shutterstock, 84 (bottom); Photodisc, 85.

border to border · teen to teen · border to border · teen to teen · border to border